Madrid

tell us about yourself

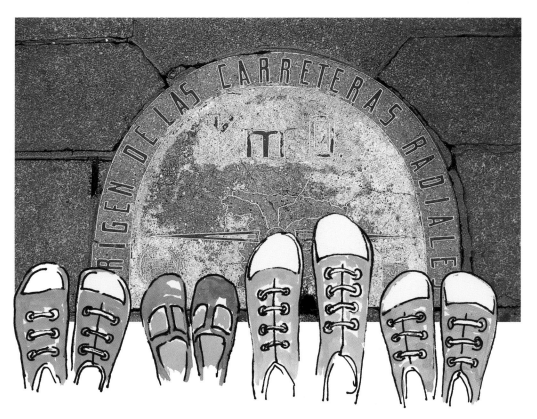

H KLICZKOWSKI

Madrid

tell us about yourself

Marta Ratti

For my daughter Verónica.
Marta Ratti

Editor: Paco Asensio

Editorial Coordinator: Aurora Cuito

Texts: Marta Ratti

Translation: Books Factory *Translations*

Illustrations: Marta Ratti

Copy Editor: Susana González

Art Director: Mireia Casanovas Soley

Graphic Design and Layout: Emma Termes Parera

Acknowledgements: Olivier Boé, Silvia and Hugo, Isabel León and Frédéric Gasc

Photographs: © Raúl Usieto, except pages 40 and 42 © All rights reserved, Museo Nacional del Prado; and pages 44, 62, 74, Celia Ciprés

Copyright for the international edition
© H Kliczkowski-Onlybook, S.L.
La Fundición, 15. Polígono Industrial Santa Ana
28529 Rivas-Vaciamadrid. Madrid
Tel.: +34 91 666 50 01
Fax: +34 91 301 26 83
onlybook@asppan.com
www.onlybook.com

Editorial Project

LOFT Publications
Via Laietana, 32 4° Of. 92
08003 Barcelona. España
Tel.: +34 932 688 088
Fax: +34 932 687 073
e-mail: loft@loftpublications.com
www.loftpublications.com

Printed in:
Gràfiques Anman. Sabadell, Spain

February 2003

ISBN: 84-96137-56-2
D.L.: B-01729-03

visit Madrid with your new friends

Vero

Sole

Tobi

Pedro

Puerta del Sol

On a sunny Sunday morning Vero, Pedro, Tobi and his sister Sole are seated on a bench in Puerta del Sol, which is a very special place in Madrid.

"What is this plaque on the ground?" Pedro asks.

The group comes closer and begins to read: "The starting point of the radial highways. Km 0".

"I know! I know!" exclaims Vero. This plaque indicates that this is where you start counting the kilometers for all of the highways in Spain. We're standing on top of kilometer zero.

What they have just found is a starting point.

"It's like in the stories when they begin 'Once upon a time…'" Pedro adds.

"Yes, starting from here, we could go visit all of the cities of the country and learn about their history, people, buildings… I've got a great idea! Why don't we start by visiting Madrid?" Vero proposes.

"Yeees!" They all chime in enthusiastically.

"But someone should help us, someone who knows the city very well, someone who can be our tour guide," thinking Tobi outloud. "My teddy bear is really smart. Maybe he would like to help us," the littlest girl says, as she shows them her teddy bear.

Suddenly, from the square, a deep voice says to them: "Is somebody calling me? Did somebody say 'bear'?"

The four friends are astonished on seeing the famous 'madroño' bear, who is the symbol of the city of Madrid, climb down from the pedestal, and walk over to them. "Woof! I've been dying to stretch my legs."

"Fantastic!" they all exclaim. "Could you help to see us around Madrid?"

"Of course," the bear replies. I know all the stories of this city, I've listened to millions of people who have passed through this square, day after day… But somebody had better take my place on top of the sculpture while I'm away."

"I'm sure my teddy bear would like to do it," Sole says.

"Well, great then! Everything is arranged. Let's go kids! Let's start with Puerta del Sol."

"It is believed that there used to be a castle here in the old days, and that it had a sun on one of its walls."

"A castle in the middle of the city?" Pedro asks.

"Well, you see in those days, this wasn't exactly the center of the city. It wasn't until the 16th century when important buildings for the life of the city, started being built around it."

"Like Casa de Correos (old postal service), which today is the Presidencia de la Comunidad de Madrid (the local goverment)."

"My daddy says that because it is so very famous, that is why everybody comes here on New Year's Eve, to eat the 12 grapes and usher in the new year."

"That's right Sole. Now, I would like to propose that we go to Plaza Mayor."

Off to Plaza Mayor.

plaza Mayor

"This plaza is enormous!"

"And that building over there. What's that?"

"It's Casa de la Panadería (old bakers' guild)," the bear says. "Together with Casa de la Carnicería (old butchers' guild), these are the only two public buildings in the plaza. The rest are residential buildings. Over the years, more than 3,500 people have lived here."

"Ooooohhhh…"

"Centuries ago, this square used to be a market. At that time, it was also used for poetry competitions, bullfights, passacaglia, theater and royal ceremonies. The nobility occupied the balconies so as to watch the spectacle."
"At Christmas time there is a fair here, and I come with my mom and dad to buy the Christmas tree and decorations."

"Are you wondering why they are called Casa de la Panadería and Casa de la Carnicería?"

"No," the children reply.

"Because it refers to the trades and jobs that were undertaken here."

"Ah! That's why the street signs have names like Botoneras (button makers) or Biombo (screen)."

"But, Lechuga (lettuce) isn't a trade," Sole points out.

"No, but in that street, all types of vegetables were sold," the bear answers.

Off to Teatro de la Ópera and Plaza de Oriente.

Teatro de la ópera

"This quarter has a long tradition of music and theater. The streets surrounding the theater Teatro de la Ópera, are full of shops that sell musical instruments," the bear explains to the children.

Palacio Real and Plaza de Oriente

"Behind the theater is Plaza de Oriente. The royal family used to stroll here, among the elegant sculptures and beautiful gardens."

"Did the royal family live near here?" Pedro asks.

"Yes, of course. In that luxurious edifice that you can see back there called Palacio Real, which was their residence during the 18th century. Now, Juan Carlos the King and Sofia the Queen live in Palacio de la Zarzuela."

"I'm tired. Can't we rest for a while?" –Vero asks.

"Yes, please. And I'm hungry, too," Sole adds.

"Well, if you'd like to have a typical chocolate with 'churros', we can go visit the Madrid 'villano'," the bear proposes to them.

"And what's that?"

"Madrid 'villano' encompasses the most ancient quarters of the city. It is teeming with legends, superstitions, old tales and fables."

off to the Madrid 'villano'.

Barrio de la Latina

"This is Plaza de la Paja (straw). In medieval times, it was the biggest square and forage was sold here. Now, as we can see, it's full of outdoor cafés and is a very popular meeting place," the bear explains. "From the narrow streets and alleys surrounding it, we can get a good idea of what this small, bustling city was like in those days."

El Rastro

"Look at all the people!" Vero exclaims.

"People flock here on Sundays, because you can buy or sell practically anything: from records to fancy antiques, and from pets to second-hand clothes. Look around and you'll see how many things there are."

Barrio de Lavapiés

"In this neighborhood, many 'chulos' and chulapas' used to live here, and still do in fact. Do you know what I mean by 'chulos'?

"Well, we know that they are very typical in Madrid."

"Many years ago, the people that lived in this area were known to all the city for their way of dressing and their sophisticated air, which earned them the name of 'chulapos'," says the bear.

"What does sophisticated mean?" asks Vero.

"Well, it refers to someone who is very educated and courteous… As I was saying, this way of behaving became very typical in Madrid, and even famous thanks to the writers of the 19th century, who represented it in many of their works. The houses where they lived were also very typical, joined by a single balcony that gave onto a common patio, called 'corralas'."

"It's very hot. Isn't there a fountain around here?"
"Come on. Let's take off these clothes. If we do, we'll be a lot cooler, and then we can go find a fountain, right bear?"

"If you like fountains then I'd like you to meet a good friend of mine. It's very near here. To get there, we can stroll along a lovely boulevard full of trees and flowers called Paseo de la Castellana."

"Great idea!" they all exclaim at once.

"I'd love to eat some candy," Sole sighs.

"Look. I have the most delicious candy in Madrid. It's called violet caramels and it's a very typical sweet of the city," the bear explains to them.

Off to Fuente de Cibeles and Fuente de Neptuno.

Suddenly, they come face to face, with an enormous sculpture
of a woman in a carriage, pulled by two lions.

"My friends, the goddess Cibeles," the bear states proudly.

"Why are the lions pulling the carriage?" Vero asks.

"Good question Vero. According to mythology, Aphrodite, the goddess of love, helped Hipomenes to win Atalanta's love. However, the young couple dared to enter the sacred temple of Cibeles, the mother of the gods of Olympus. Cibeles punished the young couple for this offense, by obliging them to pull the carriage, for all eternity."

"My dad told me that when the Real Madrid football team wins a trophy, they celebrate it here," Tobi says.

"That's right, and Atlético de Madrid, another football team in the city, does their celebrating at Fuente de Neptuno."

off to Puerta de Alcalá.

Puerta de Alcalá

"Notice everybody, that this monument has two very different sides," the bear points out.

"That's right! But why is that?" Sole enquires.

"Because Francisco Sabatini, the architect, presented King Carlos III with two projects. We don't know why, but the King chose both, so he decided to build one on each side."

Off to Museo del Prado.

Museo del prado

As they arrive in front of a majestic edifice the bear asks them:

"Do you like painting?"

"Yeah!!!" all the children respond together.

"Well, in Madrid, we have Museo del Prado, which is one of the most extensive painting collections in the world."

 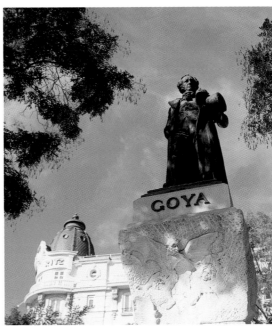

"Who are these men?"

"And what are they holding in their hands?"

"It's a painter's palette!", Pedro blurts out.

"Very good, Pedro!" the bear says. "It's the palette that painters use for mixing their colors on. These are sculptures of two of my favorite painters: Goya and Velázquez. What would you think of taking a trip in time, and looking at the paintings of other periods?"

"Fantastic!" they all shouted out in reply.

Once inside, the bear leads them to an interesting Velázquez painting.

"It's called *Las Meninas* and it's reputed to be one of the best paintings ever made," the bear explains to them.

"What is a menina?" Sole asks.

"They were the young ladies of company that served the royal family's children."

"I see. They were like the princess's friends, and that's why Velázquez painted them all together, right?"

"Exactly," the bear replied.

"There's one thing that I don't understand, though." Pedro is thinking aloud. "Why is Velázquez in his own painting?"

"We are not really sure why Velázquez put himself in this painting. In the period in which he lived, kings and queens were considered to be the center of the world, and maybe it was a desire on his part, to be included in this center."

"How did he manage to paint himself in?"

"Well, we're not really sure. This painting is full of enigmas."

"It's fascinating."

"The dresses and the girl's hair are delightful," Sole comments.

They carry on through the museum, and they come upon a hall with Goya paintings.

"It's great! It's a painting of a party, isn't it?" the children cry out.

"That's right. In these works Goya shows us the customs of the common man, their parties, their habits –the bear explains."

"I see. Velázquez painted the royalty, and Goya their subjects."

"Ha, ha! Something like that," the bear replied laughingly.

"OK, kids. What would you think about going to visit the biggest park in the city? We can take the bus which will leave us off at the main gate."
"All right!"

Off to Parque del Retiro.

Parque del Retiro

While the bear rows them around the magnificent pond, the children are fascinated by all the birds and fish that come up to the boat. The bear explains that this park was designed so that the king and queen had a place where they could rest and think.

"Oh, so kids couldn't come here and play before?" Vero asks.

"No, they couldn't, but fortunately now, it belongs to the city of Madrid, and it's available for all the citizens to enjoy."

With nature all around them in the park, the children are delighted. They enjoy the sun, the flowers…

...the trees and the shade. The Parque del Retiro is the green lung of Madrid. Here one can climb trees, play hide-and-seek, tag, ball and also find out the names of the different plant species that live in it.

They pay a visit to Palacio de Cristal (glass). In the past it was a greenhouse, but nowadays, it is used for art exhibitions.

"We've seen where the king and queen rest. Now, follow me, and we can discover some other things," the bear says.

"It's just occurred to me that maybe we could pay a visit to the most popular street in the city. It's full of cinemas, theaters and shops," the bear points out.

"Yes! Yes! Take us there. We can take the subway to get there even faster," Tobi suggests.

Off to Gran Vía.

Gran Vía

"It took 44 years to finish building this avenue. It was modeled after main avenues in other important cities around the world —the bear comments—. Notice the big billboards. It's one of the few cities in the world where they are still painted by hand. It's unusual, isn't it?"

"And what about that white building?"

"That's the Telefónica building, the first skyscraper in Madrid."

"Hey, bear. Are the Don Quijote and Sancho Panza statues near here?" Vero asks.

"Yes, of course. They're in Plaza España, which is very near. Would you all like to see them?"

"You bet! Let's go!"

"This sculpture is dedicated to Miguel de Cervantes, the author of the famous novel *Don Quijote*. Don Quijote was a knight who wore armor and carried a long lance. Together with his squire, Sancho Panza, they lived all kinds of adventures in search of Quijote's lover, Dulcinea. One time, he even got into a fight with the windmills, because he thought they were his enemies."

"If you look at the buildings behind them, you'll notice that they are also a representation of this unusual, odd couple."

"Ah, I see. One is tall and thin."

"Oh, yes, and the other is short and plumpy."

"Ha, ha! How funny!"

After telling his story, the bear is quiet for a moment, as he stops to think. Then, he gets up, and with his paintbrush, he surprises the children again. "And now, we are going to go to Egypt! What do you all think about that?" "Wonderful!" all the children cry out at once.

Off to Templo de Debod.

Templo de Debod

"This Egyptian temple was brought directly from the banks of the Nile River. Egypt gave it to Spain as a gift, to thank them for the help afforded in the construction of a dam at Aswan. In the second century BC, King Adijalamani ordered the construction of the original temple in honor of Amon and Isis. Authentic Egyptian paintings depict-ing offerings to the gods, are preserved in the interior."

"Thanks a million for this unforgettable tour," the children told him gratefully.

"Hold on! We haven't finished yet. I've been reserving one last surprise for you all. Are you ready for it?" the bear said as he smiled.

Then, he took out his magical paintbrush, and started to
paint a huge balloon full of colors.
The children stared dumbfounded, as they watch the bear
finish the painting.

A gift from the bear

"And now, my dear friends, the best of the show is about to begin. We are going to see the sky of Madrid which is the delight of both those who live here, and those who come to visit. Open your eyes wide because this is almost a painting, even though you won't find it in a museum."

The bear and the children affectionately bid each other farewell, and they promise to meet again, to continue with their adventures. The bear gives each of them an album of postcards, of the beautiful places in Madrid, that they still have to visit.

Album

FOTOS

Ta da!

Puerta de Europa.

¡Hala, Madrid! ¡Hala, Madrid! is the hymn of the Real Madrid.

Toot toot!

The old Atocha station is now a tropical garden.

I look like a real-life bullfighter, don't I? This is Plaza de las Ventas, up to 23,000 people can watch me perform!

We still haven't been to many of the parks in Madrid:

La Casa de Campo, el Pardo, Aranjuez...

The zoo, where my friends live.

And Sole's teddy?

When they return to the plaza, they find Sole's teddy bear at the foot of the 'madroño' monument.

"Thanks for helping out our friend. It's time to go home teddy bear," Sole says as she holds him affectionately.
"See you soon, bear!"

le Alcalá

Visit Madrid

1. Puerta del Sol
2. Plaza Mayor
3. Teatro de la Ópera
4. Palacio Real
5. Plaza de Oriente
6. Plaza de la Paja
7. El Rastro
8. Barrio de Lavapiés
9. Fuentes de Cibeles y Neptuno
10. Puerta de Alcalá
11. Estadio Vicente Calderón
12. Parque del Retiro
13. Estadio Santiago Bernabeu
14. Atocha station
15. Museo del Prado
16. Museo Nacional Centro de Arte Reina Sofía
17. Museo Thyssen-Bornemisza
18. Templo de Debod
19. Plaza España
20. Barrio de la Latina

La Fundición, 15 Poligono Industrial Santa Ana 28529 Rivas-Vaciamadrid Madrid Tel. 34 91 666 50 01 Fax 34 91 301 26 83 asppan@asppan.com www.onlybook.com

Barcelona, explica'ns Gaudí/Barcelona, cuéntanos de Gaudí/
Barcelona, tell us about Gaudí
ISBN: (C)   84-89439-32-X
ISBN: (E)   84-89439-29-X
ISBN: (GB) 84-89439-28-1

Barcelona, parla'ns de tu/Barcelona, cuéntanos de ti/
Barcelona, tell us about yourself
ISBN: (C)   84-96048-34-9
ISBN: (E)   84-96048-33-0
ISBN: (GB) 84-96048-36-5